Warriors of the World

Written by Ben Hubbard

Illustrated by Mat Edwards

Contents

Collins

1 The first warriors

Warriors have existed since the start of human history. Thousands of years ago, when tribes focused on hunting and gathering, people had to protect their tribes. They were given weapons such as stone axes and wooden clubs when they were old enough to fight. These people formed fighting bands. They were the first warriors.

Over time, hunters and gatherers settled in one place, where they built a village, town or city. This created **civilisations** where young warriors were trained to fight with iron weapons and armour. Groups of warriors developed their own fighting techniques and rules, which always included honour, loyalty and fearlessness in war.

Some warrior groups built powerful reputations which we still remember today. This book is all about these warriors and the cultures and countries they came from. They are history's most famous warriors.

2 The Spartans

Three thousand years ago, the Spartans were the world's most fearsome fighting machines. As young children, Spartan boys spent every moment training for war. At seven years old, they were sent away to city camps and taught to fight. Life there was harsh. The boys were kept hungry and cold to toughen them up. They had to steal food to survive but were whipped if they were caught. By the age of 20, each Spartan man was a hardened warrior who was ready to die for Sparta.

Greek city-states

Ancient Greece was formed of hundreds of city-states, and Sparta was one of them. Each city-state was like a small country, with its own government and army. Sometimes, Greek city-states fought against each other. At other times, they joined together to fight an outside enemy, such as the **Persians**.

Mysterious myth

Male Spartan babies who seemed weak were killed as soon as they were born. It was said these babies were thrown from Mount Taygetos, Sparta's highest and most important mountain. However, no bones have ever been found there. It's likely that the babies were simply left outside homes to die.

The ruins of Sparta

1000 BCE

1000 BCE:
Sparta founded.

700 BCE
600 BCE
500 BCE
400 BCE
300 BCE
200 BCE
100 BCE
0 CE
100 CE
200 CE
300 CE
400 CE
500 CE
600 CE
700 CE
800 CE
900 CE
1000 CE
1100 CE
1200 CE
1300 CE
1400 CE
1500 CE
1600 CE
1700 CE
1800 CE
1900 CE
2000 CE

5

Into battle

Spartan warriors were famous for their long hair, crimson cloaks and marching into battle singing war songs.

Spartan warrior

Corinthian helmet

bronze cuirass
(chest and
back armour)

long curved
kopis sword

sandals

shield
painted with (Λ),
the symbol for Sparta

short double-edged
xiphos sword

leg greaves
(guards)

Fearsome feat

In the 4th century BCE, the Spartans decided not to use most of their armour in battle and wore only leg greaves, helmets and cloaks. This made them faster and more flexible.

Phalanx formation

The Spartans fought in a battle formation used by all Greek armies, called a *phalanx*. This was made up of at least eight rows of warriors. In the front row, the warriors locked their shields together to form a wall. Then they thrust their spears at the enemy through the gaps. If the phalanx broke, the warriors fought with their swords in one-to-one combat.

1000 BCE
900 BCE
800 BCE
700 BCE
600 BCE
500 BCE

500 BCE: Sparta becomes a military city-state.

100 BCE
0 CE
100 CE
200 CE
300 CE
400 CE
500 CE
600 CE
700 CE
800 CE
900 CE
1000 CE
1100 CE
1200 CE
1300 CE
1400 CE
1500 CE
1600 CE
1700 CE
1800 CE
1900 CE
2000 CE

King Leonidas's last stand

This famous Spartan king made a heroic last stand against an invading Persian army. Leonidas and 300 Spartans fought off tens of thousands of Persian soldiers at a small mountain pass at Thermopylae, in central Greece. The Spartans stopped the Persians invading for two whole days, but were finally defeated after bravely fighting to the last man. A group of Greek city-states later defeated the Persians.

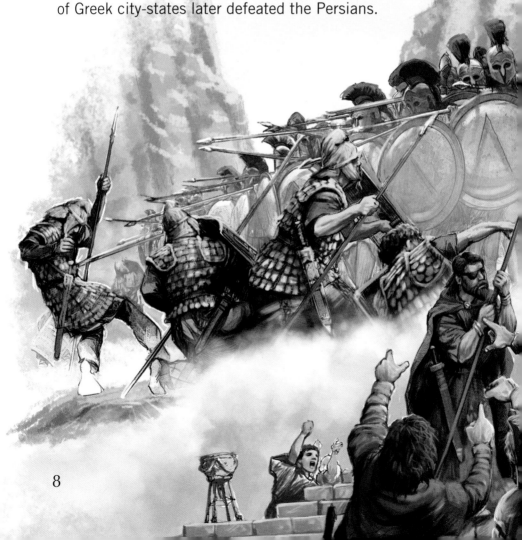

Two Spartan warriors at the Battle of Thermopylae were Aristodemus and Eurytus. Both had been blinded by an eye disease and King Leonidas ordered them back to Sparta. But instead of leaving, Eurytus put on his armour and joined the battle. Aristodemus travelled to Sparta alone. Once home, Aristodemus was branded a coward and no one would speak to him. He tried to make things better by fighting bravely in another battle against the Persians, but failed, with the Spartans saying his fighting was too reckless.

Tall tale

The ancient historian Herodotus said the Persian army at Thermopylae numbered over two million men. Today's historians say it was more likely to be between 70,000 and 300,000.

1000 BCE
900 BCE
800 BCE
700 BCE
600 BCE
500 BCE
400 BCE

480 BCE: Battle of Thermopylae

200 BCE
100 BCE
0 CE
100 CE
200 CE
300 CE
400 CE
500 CE
600 CE
700 CE
800 CE
900 CE
1000 CE
1100 CE
1200 CE
1300 CE
1400 CE
1500 CE
1600 CE
1700 CE
1800 CE
1900 CE
2000 CE

3 The Celts

Centuries after the Spartans' battle at Thermopylae, fierce
new fighters broke on to Europe's battlefields – the Celts.
Many believed them to be the world's wildest warriors.
Tall, tattooed and terrifying, Celts painted themselves blue and
spiked up their hair with **white lime**. Some even fought naked.
These Celtic warriors yelled, chanted and blew horns
before battle. To an army facing them, the Celts seemed
like mad beasts.

Who were the Celts?

The Celts were a people of many tribes living across Europe between 2000 BCE and 100 CE. The Celts were not united, but shared a similar culture, language and fighting techniques. Many Celtic tribes moved to different countries over time. They would either settle peacefully or take land by force. Some tribes lived in hill forts protected by fences and ditches.

Tall tale

As the invaders of their lands, the Romans were the Celts' enemies. They described the Celts as hairy, naked **barbarians** who lived to drink and fight. But **runes** and **artefacts** show us there was more to the Celts. They were great jewellers, craftsmen and **bards**. For example, this bronze shield was found in the River Thames, London.

1000 BCE
900 BCE

900s BCE: Celts migrate to Western Europe.

500 BCE
400 BCE
300 BCE
200 BCE
100 BCE
0 CE
100 CE
200 CE
300 CE
400 CE
500 CE
600 CE
700 CE
800 CE
900 CE
1000 CE
1100 CE
1200 CE
1300 CE
1400 CE
1500 CE
1600 CE
1700 CE
1800 CE
1900 CE
2000 CE

The charge of the Celts

Celts did not march into battle in formation, like the Spartans. Instead, they charged wildly with their long, slashing swords held high and hacked at anything in their way. Most Celts fought on foot, but the chiefs rode into battle aboard war **chariots**. Battle was a chance for warriors to show off their bravery and skills and to become the subject of a bard's poem.

Celtic warrior

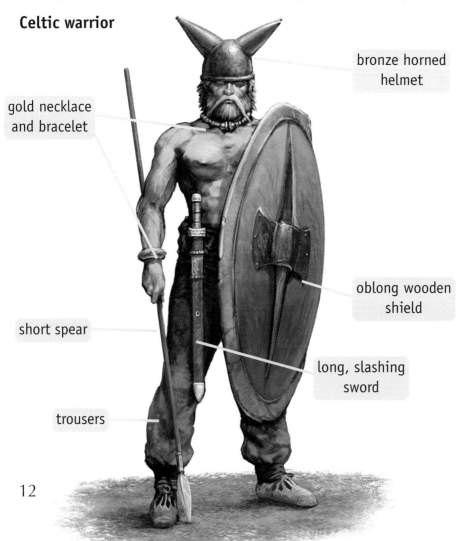

bronze horned helmet

gold necklace and bracelet

oblong wooden shield

short spear

long, slashing sword

trousers

Battles at dawn

Celtic tribes sometimes fought each other over land or because of an argument. Their armies arranged to face each other as the sun rose. The warriors shouted insults, beat their shields and fought to the death. Sometimes, small groups would fight and the outcome of these mini-battles often decided the overall winner. At other times, a full-scale battle erupted between the armies.

Fearsome feat

In 52 BCE, Celtic chief Vercingetorix won a famous victory against Roman general Julius Caesar and his mighty **legions** at the Battle of Gergovia. However, Caesar then defeated Vercingetorix at the Battle of Alesia and invaded all of Gaul (modern-day France).

1000 BCE
900 BCE
800 BCE
700 BCE
600 BCE
500 BCE
400 BCE
300 BCE
200 BCE
100 BCE
0 CE

52 BCE: Celts beat the Romans at the Battle of Gergovia

400 CE
500 CE
600 CE
700 CE
800 CE
900 CE
1000 CE
1100 CE
1200 CE
1300 CE
1400 CE
1500 CE
1600 CE
1700 CE
1800 CE
1900 CE
2000 CE

13

Queen Boudica

Queen Boudica was married to Prasutagus, king of
the Celtic Iceni tribe. Prasutagus was an **ally** to the Romans.
But everything changed when Prasutagus died. The Romans
invaded the Iceni land, whipped Boudica and attacked
her daughters. Boudica promised she would not rest until she
had taken revenge.

In 61 CE, Boudica gathered a Celtic army to invade the cities
of Camulodunum (modern-day Colchester), Verulamium
(St Albans) and London. The Celts murdered the people
and set the cities alight. The army then destroyed an entire
Roman legion. But the Romans struck back, and Boudica
was beaten in the Celt's last desperate battle.
She took poison rather than be captured.
Boudica is remembered as one of Britain's
bravest heroes.

14

Mysterious myth

The Celts believed a person's head could live on, even if it was parted from their body. Celtic warriors would often cut off their enemies' heads and put them on display as trophies.

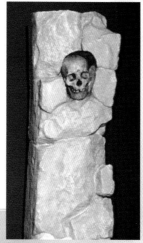

1000 BCE
900 BCE
800 BCE
700 BCE
600 BCE
500 BCE
400 BCE
300 BCE
200 BCE
100 BCE
0 CE
100 CE

61 CE: Boudica defeated at the Battle of Watling Street.

500 CE
600 CE
700 CE
800 CE
900 CE
1000 CE
1100 CE
1200 CE
1300 CE
1400 CE
1500 CE
1600 CE
1700 CE
1800 CE
1900 CE
2000 CE

4 The Vikings

Many years after the Celts disappeared, **seafaring** warriors from Denmark, Norway and Sweden burst on to the shores of Europe. These were the Vikings: raiders and invaders who terrorised Europe for over 300 years. During their raids on settlements, Viking warriors stole silver, slaughtered many people and enslaved others. A Viking's main aim in life was to fight, and to gain fame and fortune. They wanted to be remembered long after their death.

The Viking longship

The Vikings first appeared to the rest of the world when a longship full of warriors raided a monastery at Lindisfarne, northern England. The Vikings would have been nothing without their longships, which were built with both sails and oars to travel at speed and ambush settlements.

Mysterious myth

Vikings were said to use a "Sun Stone" to navigate across the sea. The sun was supposed to shine through the stone and show which direction was north. However, no such stone has ever been found, and many believe it is a myth.

—1000 BCE
— 900 BCE
— 800 BCE
— 700 BCE
— 600 BCE
— 500 BCE
— 400 BCE
— 300 BCE
— 200 BCE
— 100 BCE
— 0 CE
— 100 CE
— 200 CE
— 300 CE
— 400 CE
— 500 CE
— 600 CE
— 700 CE
— 800 CE

793 CE: Vikings raid the monastery at Lindisfarne.

1100 CE
—1200 CE
—1300 CE
—1400 CE
—1500 CE
—1600 CE
—1700 CE
—1800 CE
—1900 CE
—2000 CE

Raids and battles

Young Viking warriors had to show what they were made of
while out on their first raid. These raids involved fighting
opponents in close combat. Larger "pitched" battles
sometimes took place between armies. Before a battle began,
Vikings shouted, howled and clattered their weapons against
their shields. Then a front line of warriors formed a wall
of overlapping shields and thrust their weapons through
the gaps. When the shield wall fell apart, the warriors fought
hand-to-hand.

Viking warrior

helmet

shield

chainmail coat

sword

"bearded" axe

A Viking's weapons were his prized possessions. Vikings fought with axes, spears, and bows and arrows, but only the richest warriors could afford a sword. Great swords carried by famous warriors were given names such as "Leg Biter", "Life Taker" and "War Flame".

Fearsome feat

The fiercest Vikings were called *berserkers*.

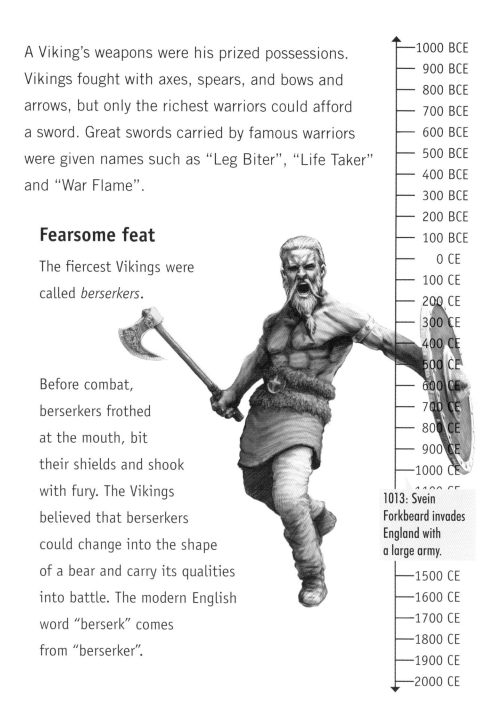

Before combat, berserkers frothed at the mouth, bit their shields and shook with fury. The Vikings believed that berserkers could change into the shape of a bear and carry its qualities into battle. The modern English word "berserk" comes from "berserker".

1000 BCE
900 BCE
800 BCE
700 BCE
600 BCE
500 BCE
400 BCE
300 BCE
200 BCE
100 BCE
0 CE
100 CE
200 CE
300 CE
400 CE
500 CE
600 CE
700 CE
800 CE
900 CE
1000 CE

1013: Svein Forkbeard invades England with a large army.

1500 CE
1600 CE
1700 CE
1800 CE
1900 CE
2000 CE

19

Hairy Britches

Ragnar Lothbrok was one of the most famous Vikings. In 845 CE, Ragnar led a **fleet** of longships up the River Seine to attack Paris. The Parisians bribed him with silver to go away. He then attacked Northumbria, in England, but was captured by its king, Aella, who tried to kill Ragnar by throwing him into a pit of snakes. But Ragnar's thick trousers stopped the snakes biting him, and he was given the nickname "Hairy Britches".

Seeing that Ragnar was not dead, Aella had him pulled up, stripped and thrown back into the snake pit. As Ragnar was bitten to death, he shouted that his sons – Halfdan and Ivar the Boneless – would seek revenge. This they did in 865 CE, when they invaded Northumbria with a great army and killed Aella.

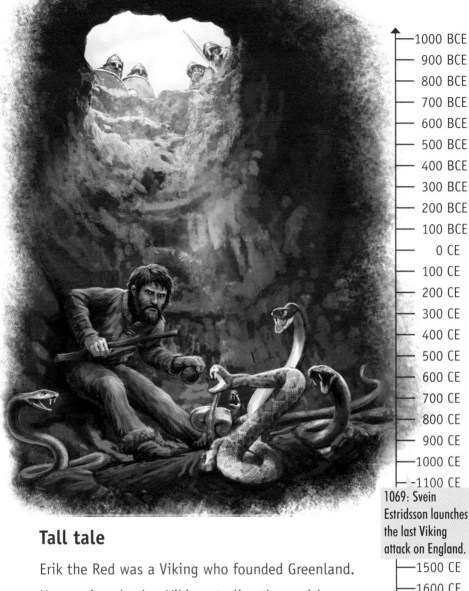

1000 BCE
900 BCE
800 BCE
700 BCE
600 BCE
500 BCE
400 BCE
300 BCE
200 BCE
100 BCE
0 CE
100 CE
200 CE
300 CE
400 CE
500 CE
600 CE
700 CE
800 CE
900 CE
1000 CE
-1100 CE

1069: Svein Estridsson launches the last Viking attack on England.

1500 CE
1600 CE
1700 CE
1800 CE
1900 CE
2000 CE

Tall tale

Erik the Red was a Viking who founded Greenland.
He convinced other Vikings to live there with
him by giving it the attractive name "Greenland".
However, it wasn't green at all, but cold and icy.

21

5 Medieval knights

Following the Viking Age, armoured horsemen came to the battlefields of Medieval Europe. These were knights: warriors clad from head to toe in suits of plated armour. It took years of training to become a knight. Young **nobles** served as castle **page boys** to learn about hunting, music and **chivalry**. At 12, a page became a squire – a knight's assistant – and began his weapons' training.

Tournament training

Knights were taught to seek glory and honour on the battlefield and had to serve their lord or king during war. In times of peace, knights practised their skills by travelling to tournaments, where armies of knights fought in mock battles called "melees", and captured each other for **ransom** money. Melees were followed by jousts, where two knights tried to unhorse each other with **lances**. The victor won horses, money and the love of the crowd.

1000 BCE
900 BCE
800 BCE
700 BCE
600 BCE
500 BCE
400 BCE
300 BCE
200 BCE
100 BCE
0 CE
100 CE
200 CE
300 CE
400 CE
500 CE
600 CE
700 CE
800 CE
900 CE
1000 CE
1100 CE
-1200 CE

12th century: Tournaments for knights become popular in Europe.

1600 CE
1700 CE
1800 CE
1900 CE
2000 CE

Tall tale

Medieval knights were supposed to be honest, brave and fair under a code of honour called chivalry. But many were not. Some dishonest knights used sharp instead of blunt weapons during tournaments, which caused injury and death.

Knights in armour

Early knights wore suits of linked rings called chainmail.
But over time this changed to plate armour, which covered
a knight from head to foot, completed by a helmet with a visor
or eye slits. A knight in armour was well protected from enemy
arrows, swords and lances. However, full suits of armour were
heavy, especially when holding a broadsword and large shield.

Knight in armour

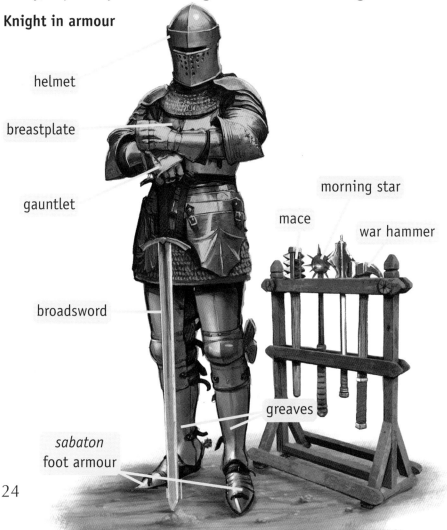

helmet

breastplate

gauntlet

morning star

mace

war hammer

broadsword

greaves

sabaton
foot armour

Mysterious myth

Many medieval ideas about chivalry came from the tales of King Arthur. Arthur was a legendary king who led a round table of knights and had a sword with special powers, Excalibur. Nobody knows if Arthur really existed.

Mounted charge

A mounted knight was a formidable opponent, especially against foot soldiers. During battle, knights led charges towards the enemy, before dismounting to fight on foot with a hand weapon for one-on-one combat. A knight wore a **coat of arms** to show their identity. Killing an important enemy gave the knight glory and respect.

1000 BCE
900 BCE
800 BCE
700 BCE
600 BCE
500 BCE
400 BCE
300 BCE
200 BCE
100 BCE
0 CE
100 CE
200 CE
300 CE
400 CE
500 CE
600 CE
700 CE
800 CE
900 CE
1000 CE
1100 CE
1200 CE
1300 CE
-1400 CE

14th century: Plate armour replaces chainmail.

1700 CE
1800 CE
1900 CE
2000 CE

The First Knight

English nobleman William Marshal was known as "the greatest knight who ever lived". Born in 1146, Marshal was an expert in war and tournaments. At his first tournament, the 20 year old captured four knights for ransom in the melee: a high total for any knight. He regularly attended tournaments, which won him fame and fortune.

Fearsome feat

He might have been famous, but William Marshal still used dirty tricks to win prizes at tournaments. Instead of capturing a knight by fighting him, Marshal sometimes sneakily rode up beside him and grabbed the reins from his opponent's hands.

Marshal soon became known as the "First Knight", because he was considered the most important knight in the land. Marshal went on to serve four English kings: Henry II, Richard I, John and Henry III. John was such a bad king that many nobles rebelled against him. However, Marshal helped stop this and forced John to sign a document called the Magna Carta. This was a **charter** of rights which said the king could no longer rule with absolute power.

— 1000 BCE
— 900 BCE
— 800 BCE
— 700 BCE
— 600 BCE
— 500 BCE
— 400 BCE
— 300 BCE
— 200 BCE
— 100 BCE
— 0 CE
— 100 CE
— 200 CE
— 300 CE
— 400 CE
— 500 CE
— 600 CE
— 700 CE
— 800 CE
— 900 CE
— 1000 CE
— 1100 CE
— 1200 CE
— 1300 CE
— 1400 CE
— 1500 CE
— 1600 CE

16th century: Firearms make knights in armour redundant.

— 2000 CE

The tomb of William Marshall

6 The Samurai

Away from the battlefields of Europe, a different type of mounted warrior emerged – the samurai. These were Japan's **elite** warriors: swordsmen who trained for their whole lives in the art of war. They learnt archery, horsemanship and sword fighting from five years old. At 15, they were given an adult name, armour and a samurai sword, called a *katana* – a samurai's most prized possession, which would only leave their side in death.

Way of the warrior

Samurai lived by an honour code called *bushido*, meaning "way of the warrior". The rules of bushido said:

A samurai must be loyal to his master.

A samurai must be ready to fight to the death.

A samurai must be fair, honest and polite

Who were the samurai?

Samurai means "to serve", and the first samurai warriors served the emperor of Japan as soldiers. But over time, samurai clans took control of the country for themselves. In 1185 CE, Minamoto Yoritomo of the Minamoto clan made himself Japan's military ruler. Samurai clans then governed Japan for over 700 years.

Fearsome feat

A samurai who was defeated, trapped in battle or disgraced in some way was expected to take his own life by cutting open his belly. Called *seppuku*, this was considered one of the most painful ways to die, and was therefore seen as honourable. Samurai warriors also sometimes performed seppuku after a leader was killed, following them into death.

1000 BCE
900 BCE
800 BCE
700 BCE
600 BCE
500 BCE
400 BCE
300 BCE
200 BCE
100 BCE
0 CE
100 CE
200 CE
300 CE
400 CE
500 CE
600 CE
700 CE
800 CE

8th century CE: Early samurai emerge as the emperor's soldiers.

1200 CE
1300 CE
1400 CE
1500 CE
1600 CE
1700 CE
1800 CE
1900 CE
2000 CE

29

Samurai duels

Traditionally, samurai warriors fought each other on horseback. During battle, a samurai called out their rank, family name and achievements. An enemy samurai of equal position answered their challenge and they fired arrows at each other. If neither warrior was killed, they dismounted and fought to the death with katanas. A duel between two great warriors sometimes caused the others fighting to pause, as samurai from both sides stopped to watch.

Samurai warrior

kabuto helmet

mempo mask

composite bow

body armour

wakizashi dagger

katana sword

Tall tale

Dohaku was a famous samurai who had his head cut off during a duel. However, according to legend, Dohaku found his head and a doctor successfully reattached it.

Samurai weapons

The *katana* was famous for its strength and sharpness and each one took expert sword makers weeks to create. But in the 16th century, a Portuguese trading boat introduced a new weapon to Japan: the *arquebus*. This was an early rifle which gave a simple foot soldier the power to kill a samurai warrior who had spent decades in training. It went against samurai ideals of being heroic and honourable, yet the *arquebus* became widely used in samurai warfare.

1000 BCE
900 BCE
800 BCE
700 BCE
600 BCE
500 BCE
400 BCE
300 BCE
200 BCE
100 BCE
0 CE
100 CE
200 CE
300 CE
400 CE
500 CE
600 CE
700 CE
800 CE
900 CE
1000 CE
1100 CE
1200 CE
1300 CE
1400 CE
1500 CE
-1600 CE

1543: The *arquebus* is introduced to Japan.

1900 CE
2000 CE

31

Tomoe Gozen

Tomoe Gozen was one of the few samurai women recorded in history. But she was a match for any male samurai. Tomoe was so skilled with a sword and bow that it was said she was worth 1,000 warriors. She was such a gifted rider that no horse could throw her. Tomoe was among a handful of elite samurai who rode with the famous general Minamoto Yoshinaka. Tomoe protected Yoshinaka with great fearlessness and loyalty. But she could not prevent his death in war during the 1184 Battle of Awazu.

Towards the end of this battle, Yoshinaka and five of his elite samurai, including Tomoe, were left surrounded by the enemy. Tomoe swore she would stand by Yoshinaka until the end, but he ordered her to go. Tomoe rode away, pulling an enemy samurai from his horse as she went. But when she heard that Yoshinaka had been killed, she committed seppuku as a sign of her loyalty. This was the samurai's way.

Mysterious myth

In 1281, the Mongols, warriors from Mongolia and China, tried to invade Japan. But their navy was destroyed in a terrible storm. The samurai called this storm *kamikaze,* or "divine wind".

1000 BCE
900 BCE
800 BCE
700 BCE
600 BCE
500 BCE
400 BCE
300 BCE
200 BCE
100 BCE
0 CE
100 CE
200 CE
300 CE
400 CE
500 CE
600 CE
700 CE
800 CE
900 CE
1000 CE
1100 CE
1200 CE
1300 CE
1400 CE

1877: Saigo Takamori "the last samurai" is killed in battle.

1800 CE
1900 CE
2000 CE

33

7 Aztec warriors

Like the samurai in Japan, the Aztec warriors developed for hundreds of years away from the eyes of the rest of the world. The Aztecs peaked between 1325 and 1519, when its army **conquered** a vast area across Central America. The people who'd been conquered had to provide foods, precious goods and prisoners to the Aztec ruler in Tenochtitlan, the Aztec capital. The prisoners were used as human sacrifices.

Warrior training

At birth, male Aztecs were given a small shield and spear to hold. At ten, Aztec boys were sent to warrior schools and began weapons' training at the age of 15. At 20, an Aztec warrior entered his first battle, the main aim being to capture prisoners. Once his first prisoner was captured, a warrior could cut off a boyhood lock of hair at the back of the head called a *piochtli*.

Different warriors are shown in this Aztec book, called a **codex**.

Mysterious myth

The Aztecs believed that if they did not keep spilling human blood then the sun would stop shining and the world would plunge into darkness.

1000 BCE
900 BCE
800 BCE
700 BCE
600 BCE
500 BCE
400 BCE
300 BCE
200 BCE
100 BCE
0 CE
100 CE
200 CE
300 CE
400 CE
500 CE
600 CE
700 CE
800 CE
900 CE
1000 CE
1100 CE
1200 CE
1300 CE

1325: The Aztec capital Tenochtitlan is founded.

1700 CE
1800 CE
1900 CE
2000 CE

Aztec ranks

Aztec warriors could rise through the military ranks by capturing prisoners in war. Higher ranked Aztecs were allowed to wear certain items, such as feather headdresses, cloaks and jewellery. Eagle and Jaguar warriors were among the highest ranks. Eagle warriors could wear suits made from eagle feathers and an eagle-head helmet. Jaguar warriors wore whole suits made from jaguar skin. Both Eagle and Jaguar warriors used a weapon called the *macuahuitl*, a wooden club fitted with razor-sharp pieces of volcanic glass.

Jaguar and Eagle warriors

macuahuitl club

wooden shield

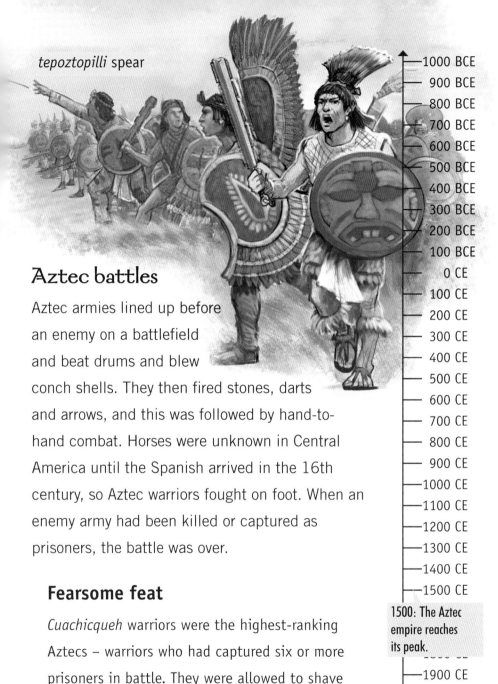

tepoztopilli spear

Aztec battles

Aztec armies lined up before an enemy on a battlefield and beat drums and blew conch shells. They then fired stones, darts and arrows, and this was followed by hand-to-hand combat. Horses were unknown in Central America until the Spanish arrived in the 16th century, so Aztec warriors fought on foot. When an enemy army had been killed or captured as prisoners, the battle was over.

Fearsome feat

Cuachicqueh warriors were the highest-ranking Aztecs – warriors who had captured six or more prisoners in battle. They were allowed to shave their heads and were known as "the shorn ones".

1000 BCE
900 BCE
800 BCE
700 BCE
600 BCE
500 BCE
400 BCE
300 BCE
200 BCE
100 BCE
0 CE
100 CE
200 CE
300 CE
400 CE
500 CE
600 CE
700 CE
800 CE
900 CE
1000 CE
1100 CE
1200 CE
1300 CE
1400 CE
1500 CE

1500: The Aztec empire reaches its peak.

1900 CE
2000 CE

Ahuitzotl the Conqueror

Born in 1440 CE, Ahuitzotl was a famous warrior king who conquered more land than any other Aztec ruler. He also demanded more goods and prisoners from his conquered people than ever before. He killed these prisoners – more than 20,000 – over four days. But Ahuitzotl's rule did not last. He was killed by a falling stone while trying to escape a flood at Tenochtitlan. Ahuitzotl's nephew Montezuma II became the next, and last, Aztec ruler.

Spanish invasion

The first Spanish army arrived in Tenochtitlan in 1519, and Montezuma II greeted their leader, Hernán Cortés, warmly. But after a few months, war between the Spanish and Aztecs broke out. This ended in the murder of Montezuma II, the **fall** of Tenochtitlan and the destruction of the Aztec Empire.

1000 BCE
900 BCE
800 BCE
700 BCE
600 BCE
500 BCE
400 BCE
300 BCE
200 BCE
100 BCE
0 CE
100 CE
200 CE
300 CE
400 CE
500 CE
600 CE
700 CE
800 CE
900 CE
1000 CE
1100 CE
1200 CE
1300 CE
1400 CE
1500 CE
1800 CE
1900 CE
2000 CE

1502: Ahuitzotl is killed.

Tall tale

Sometimes a person taken prisoner by the Aztecs was chained to a large rock and told he could win his freedom *if* he first defeated four Jaguar and Eagle warriors. Few prisoners succeeded.

8 The Sioux

The Sioux tribes were Native American people who shared a similar language, customs and beliefs. From the 18th century, many Sioux lived as **nomads** on the North American Great Plains, hunting buffalo, living in tepees, and fighting against other tribes.

When the Spanish conquered the Aztec empire, they introduced horses, not just to Central America but to North America too. Soon horse riding became vital in the Sioux's fighting methods. The Sioux had to fight to survive – to take control of hunting grounds and capture more horses. A Sioux warrior could also gain honour and glory this way.

Tall tale

To the outside world, Sioux warriors did little but hunt and fight. But this was a myth. In fact, some Sioux men chose to take on roles such as cooking and bringing up children. They were known as *winkte*, or "like a woman", and held as much respect in a tribe as the warriors.

1000 BCE
900 BCE
800 BCE
700 BCE
600 BCE
500 BCE
400 BCE
300 BCE
200 BCE
100 BCE
0 CE
100 CE
200 CE
300 CE
400 CE
500 CE
600 CE
700 CE
800 CE
900 CE
1000 CE
1100 CE
1200 CE
1300 CE
1400 CE
1500 CE
1600 CE

1600s: The Sioux inhabit the Great Plains area.

2000 CE

41

The Sioux attack

Sioux warriors were expert horsemen who fired their bows with deadly accuracy during attacks. They then dismounted their horses to fight with clubs, tomahawks and knives. Knives were used to cut off an enemy's **scalp**.

Sioux warrior

headdress

composite bow

tomahawk

knife

stone club

Fearsome feat

During the 1860s, many Sioux warriors fought against Europeans who were trying to take over their land. The US army was so scared of the Sioux chief Red Cloud that they signed a peace **treaty** with him. This was the only treaty ever signed with a Native American chief.

The Sioux usually either raided or led a surprise attack on a settlement. But sometimes two Sioux armies met for a battle. When this happened, the two sides tried not to kill too many warriors. This was because Sioux birth rates were low and lives were seen as precious. As a result, their combat sometimes looked like sport. Warriors won points for stealing horses or touching enemy warriors with a wooden **coup stick**.

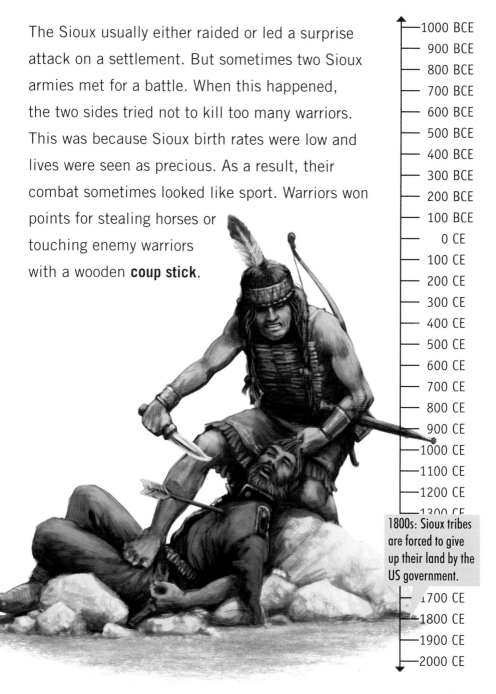

1000 BCE
900 BCE
800 BCE
700 BCE
600 BCE
500 BCE
400 BCE
300 BCE
200 BCE
100 BCE
0 CE
100 CE
200 CE
300 CE
400 CE
500 CE
600 CE
700 CE
800 CE
900 CE
1000 CE
1100 CE
1200 CE
1300 CE

1800s: Sioux tribes are forced to give up their land by the US government.

1700 CE
1800 CE
1900 CE
2000 CE

Sitting Bull and Little Bighorn

Born in 1838, Sitting Bull was a famous Sioux chief who fought against the US army in the 1860s and 1870s. At this time, European settlers were moving on to Sioux land. In response, the Sioux mounted attacks on European settlements and army bases. The US government, in turn, sent its army to fight the Sioux.

Sitting Bull's most famous victory was the 1876 Battle of Little Bighorn, in Montana. During the battle, US general George Custer attacked Sitting Bull's village with 700 soldiers. But he'd underestimated the number of Sitting Bull's warriors – around 2,000. In a brutal two-hour battle, George Custer, 210 of his men and 50 Sioux warriors were killed. Sitting Bull's warriors won, but the US army reacted with even more force, eventually removing the Sioux from most of their lands.

Mysterious myth

Sioux chief Crazy Horse believed he couldn't be killed in battle if he dressed plainly. This proved to be true: Crazy Horse didn't die in battle but was captured by the US army and killed while trying to escape.

1000 BCE
900 BCE
800 BCE
700 BCE
600 BCE
500 BCE
400 BCE
300 BCE
200 BCE
100 BCE
0 CE
100 CE
200 CE
300 CE
400 CE
500 CE
600 CE
700 CE
800 CE
900 CE
1000 CE
1100 CE
1200 CE
1300 CE

1890: The Wounded Knee Massacre ends the Sioux war against the US army.

1900 CE
2000 CE

9 The Zulu

The Zulu are one of the most famous warrior tribes in Africa. Originally, they were simply a Southern African tribe of cattle herdsmen, but this changed in 1807 when chief Dingiswayo decided to turn the Zulu into warriors. It meant all 18-year-old boys had to join a **regiment** and live in a **barracks**. Each regiment had its own colours and lived together for the next 20 years. To toughen up, warriors were given little to eat and encouraged to fight other regiments. Their lives were all about fighting and waiting for war.

Shaka

In 1816, the famous warrior Shaka replaced Dingiswayo as Zulu chief. Shaka used a short stabbing spear and killed any warrior who disobeyed him. During the 1820s, Shaka's warriors conquered a vast area across Southern Africa, forming the Zulu Empire. But when Shaka's mother died, he became crazy with grief. He killed thousands of his own Zulu people, including women. He was murdered in 1828.

Mysterious myth

Zulu warriors believed they would be protected in battle if they covered themselves in a potion made from plants and herbs.

1000 BCE
900 BCE
800 BCE
700 BCE
600 BCE
500 BCE
400 BCE
300 BCE
200 BCE
100 BCE
0 CE
100 CE
200 CE
300 CE
400 CE
500 CE
600 CE
700 CE
800 CE
900 CE
1000 CE
1100 CE
1200 CE
1300 CE

1709: The Zulus are founded in Southern Africa.

1700 CE
1800 CE
1900 CE
2000 CE

47

The Zulu army

Several Zulu regiments combined to create a fast-moving mobile army called an *impi*. They were accompanied by boys who carried food, sleeping maps and extra weapons. An impi could march over 30 kilometres a day to attack an enemy. In battle, an *impi* formed a buffalo horn shape. Younger warriors made up the "horns" which encircled the enemy. The "chest" of more experienced warriors moved slowly forward. The "loins" were older warriors who stood behind in reserve.

Zulu warrior

monkey-skin and feather headdress

iwisa throwing club

cattle-hide war shield

iklwa stabbing spear

assegai throwing spear

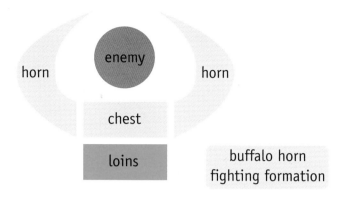

horn

enemy

horn

chest

loins

buffalo horn
fighting formation

Zulus attacked their enemy by jogging towards them while beating their shields with their spears. When they were 30 metres away, the Zulu threw their spears and then began hand-to-hand combat. The Zulus never took prisoners but simply killed everyone.

Fearsome feat

In 1879, the Zulus famously defeated the British army at the Battle of Isandlwana. However, the British **retaliated** with firepower and conquered the Zulu lands.

1000 BCE
900 BCE
800 BCE
700 BCE
600 BCE
500 BCE
400 BCE
300 BCE
200 BCE
100 BCE
0 CE
100 CE
200 CE
300 CE
400 CE
500 CE
600 CE
700 CE
800 CE
900 CE
1000 CE
1100 CE
1200 CE
1300 CE
1400 CE
1500 CE

1897: All Zulu lands are absorbed into the British Empire.

1900 CE
2000 CE

49

10 Warriors today

In the past, one-on-one combat between two warriors was common on the battlefield. It could make a warrior famous to win a duel against another great warrior.

However, the introduction of guns made battlefield duels a thing of the past. Now, a warrior who had trained their whole life with a blade could be killed by a soldier with a rifle.

Guns also changed how battles were fought. Powerful nations in Europe developed new guns in the 19th century. This gave them an unfair advantage against armies without guns.

The British Gatling gun, for example, killed thousands of Zulu warriors who were armed with spears and shields.

Yet the Zulu and Sioux both won great victories against modern gun-powered armies.

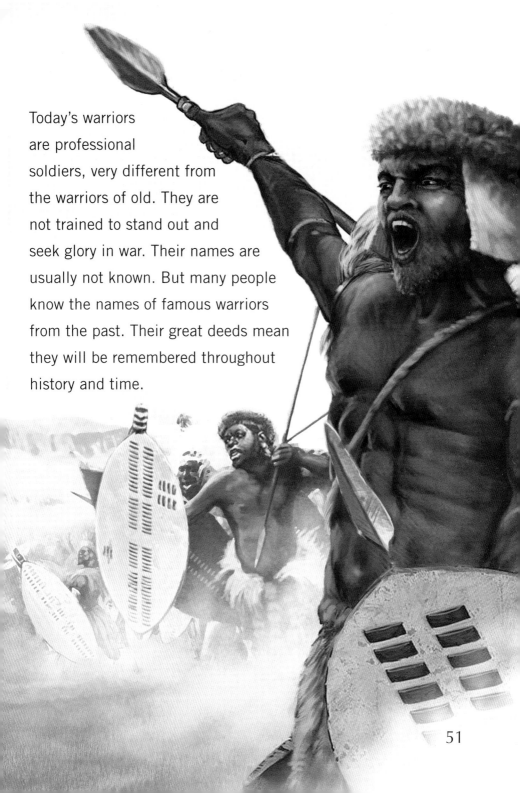

Today's warriors are professional soldiers, very different from the warriors of old. They are not trained to stand out and seek glory in war. Their names are usually not known. But many people know the names of famous warriors from the past. Their great deeds mean they will be remembered throughout history and time.

Glossary

ally a friendly country or group in war

artefacts objects made by people in the past

barbarians people from a country, group, or culture thought to be violent and uncivilised

bards poet-singers who recited stories

barracks a camp that houses soldiers

chariots two- or four-wheeled battle vehicles pulled by horses

charter a written statement describing the rights of a ruler

chivalry the qualities expected of a medieval knight: courage, honour, courtesy and justice

civilisations societies that have reached an advanced level of development

coat of arms the symbol of a person, family or country, often shown on a shield

codex an illustrated book about Aztec beliefs, customs and history, written before the European invasion

conquered gained control of a place or people through force

coup stick a stick used to count the number of blows struck against an enemy

elite a group of the best warriors or soldiers

fall capture or defeat

fleet a group of ships

lances long, pointed spears used by mounted knights

legions divisions of soldiers in the Roman army

nobles people born into the upper classes of society

nomads people that survive by travelling from place to place

page boys male servants to noblemen or knights

Persians the people of Persia, an ancient empire founded in
    what is today Iran

ransom a sum of money paid to release a prisoner

regiment a division of soldiers in an army

retaliated attacked in revenge for a similar attack

runes letters or symbols from an ancient Germanic or
    Scandinavian alphabet

scalp the skin covering the top of the head with
    the hair attached

seafaring travelling regularly by sea

treaty an agreement between two groups, armies or countries

white lime a white powder made from calcium oxide,
    a substance found in the ground

Warriors of the world battle cards

Celts

Weapons: spear; long, slashing sword

Enemies: the Romans

Famous battles: Battle of Gergovia (52 BCE), Battle of Watling Street (61 CE)

Famous warriors: Queen Boudica, Chief Vercingetorix

Aztecs

Weapons: *macuahuitl* club; *tepoztopilli* spear

Enemies: the Spanish invaders

Famous warriors: Ahuitzotl

Samurai

Weapons:
composite bow;
wakizashi dagger;
katana sword;
arquebus rifle

Famous battles:
Battle of Awazu
(1184)

Famous warriors:
Minamoto Yoritomo,
Tomoe Gozen,
Minamoto Yoshinaka

The Zulu

Weapons:
iwisa throwing club;
iklwa stabbing
spear; *assegai*
throwing spear

Enemies:
the British

Famous battles:
Battle of Isandlwana
(1879)

Ideas for reading

Written by Gill Matthews
Primary Literacy Consultant

Reading objectives:

- read books that are structured in different ways and read for a range of purposes
- check that the book makes sense to them, discussing their understanding and exploring the meaning of words in context
- retrieve, record and present information from non-fiction

Spoken language objectives:

- give well-structured descriptions, explanations and narratives for different purposes, including for expressing feelings
- participate in discussions, presentations, performances, role play/improvisations and debates

Curriculum links: History – the Roman Empire and its impact on Britain; the Viking and Anglo-Saxon struggle for the Kingdom of England to the time of Edward the Confessor; a study of an aspect or theme in British history that extends pupils' chronological knowledge beyond 1066

Interest words: combat, duel, armed, victories, glory

Resources: ICT for research, paper and pencil crayons or felt tip pens for making a poster

Build a context for reading

- Look at the front cover. Ask children what they can see. Explore their understanding of what a warrior is.
- Ask what sort of book they think this is.
- Read the blurb together. Ask children to predict what they think they will find out from the book.
- Ask where they think they will find more information about what is in the book. Explore the contents page.

Understand and apply reading strategies

- Read p2 aloud. Ask a question that will prompt children to use their scanning skills to look for a key word, e.g. What did the rules the warriors developed always include?